KHDZ

David R. Beshears

Based on the screenplay
"KHDZ"

Greybeard Publishing
Washington State

ISBN 978-0-9914327-2-1 *(print edition)*

Greybeard Publishing
P.O. Box 480
McCleary, WA 98557-0480

KHDZ

Chapter 1

The station floor of KHDZ occupied a large, cavern-like room; wherever the walls were visible shown reddish-brown, rough-hewn rock. Several small program sets for the locally produced television shows lined one wall. There was a cooking show, a morning talk show, and others. Oddly, there were no cameras.

A walkway ran along the opposite wall, emptying into hallways at both corners.

There was a small cluster of desks in the center of the room, one occupied by a middle-aged, slightly balding man with a disheveled look.

Set in a third wall was the station manager's office, made evident by the words 'Mr. Henderson Station Manager' stenciled onto the smoked glass window set in the door.

There was a small waiting area with two chairs outside the manager's office.

John Smith sat in one of the chairs, a manila folder in his lap. John was in his early thirties. He looked out of place and more than a little uncomfortable.

Troy, a three and half foot tall, gnome-like man, was sitting in the other chair. He crossed his impossibly thin, spindly legs and smiled at John. It was a friendly smile.

This made John even more uncomfortable, but he managed an awkward smile in response.

Troy finally broke the silence. "Helluva day, eh?"

John attempted another smile. He was only half successful.

"It could have gone better," he said.

Troy nodded slowly, knowingly. He let out a long, drawn out sigh. "Ah... yep."

At that moment, the station manager's door opened. Mr. Henderson stuck his head through the opening. When he saw John, he stepped fully out of his office.

He was a large, middle-aged man with an air of administrative authority about him. He looked at John with some sense of puzzlement.

"Who are you?" he asked.

John stood. "John Smith."

Mr. Henderson looked suspiciously around the station. Satisfied that everything was as it should be, at least for the moment, he turned his attention back to the newcomer.

"That a fact," he managed. "Waddya want?"

John handed Mr. Henderson the folder that he had been holding. The station manager cautiously took it, opened it and glanced at several of the pages. After a few moments' study, he silently indicated that John should step into his office.

He spoke over his shoulder before disappearing through his door.

"Get to work, Troy."

Troy stood, grinned and gave a playful salute.

"Right away, sir."

The manager's office was sparsely furnished. There was a desk and chair, several file cabinets, and a guest chair. John waited as Mr. Henderson walked around his desk, continuing to look through the contents of the folder, positioning himself finally behind his desk.

"Hmm. Wow. Tough break, Mr. Smith." He sat down, indicated the guest chair. He spoke casually as he closed the folder and tossed it onto the desk, watched John Smith sit. "Sorry about Troy. Owner's cousin."

"No problem," said John, rather noncommittally.

"So tell me, what's an associate producer, and what have I done to deserve one?"

"I don't know."

"You do know where you are…" urged Mr. Henderson.

"I guess so," said John. "But it's a mistake."

"Yeah." Mr. Henderson pointed to the folder now sitting atop his desk. "In your case, that's actually true." He warily eyed John. "Odd, really. I've never heard of such a thing."

"My luck," said John.

"Screwed up your paperwork? That's gotta suck."

"It does."

Mr. Henderson was still not completely certain about this strange turn of events. He spoke hesitantly. "So they give you to me?"

"Just until they get it straightened out. Shouldn't be too long, you think?"

"Yeah, right." Mr. Henderson pursed his lips then, breathed noisily, as if trying to decide whether to accept this unprecedented situation for what it appeared to be. "It's better than waiting, you know, *down the hall.*"

John thought he understood what that meant, but he couldn't be sure. Still, he nodded in silent agreement.

Mr. Henderson studied John a moment longer. "Associate producer, eh? You ever done any associate producing, Mr. Smith?"

John shrugged in silent answer.

"Ya' ever been involved in television?" asked Mr. Henderson.

"Was in a studio audience once."

Mr. Henderson's expression slowly shifted to: *what the hell am I supposed to do with this guy?* It hung there for several seconds before he finally came to a management decision. He slid his chair back and stood up.

"That'll have to do then, won't it?" He held out a hand and they shook. "Welcome to Hell, John Smith."

Mr. Henderson came out of his office, John following two paces behind. The station manager spoke over his shoulder without looking back. He words sounded canned and oft-repeated.

"KHDZ. Serving Hades and outlying suburbs. Broadcasting local programming 24 hours a day. Over there are several of our sets." He turned and indicated one of the passageways. "The front lobby is down that hall. It's where you came in. It's the only way in." He indicated the other passageway. "The... *you know...* is down that way."

John glanced nervously at the threshold leading to '*you know*', and quickly turned back to the center of the station floor. They walked to middle of the room, toward the one occupied desk.

Hector stood and held out his hand. "Hey," he said, half nodding.

Mr. Henderson spoke as Hector and John shook hands. "This is John Smith. He'll be associate producing for a while."

Hector looked confused.

Mr. Henderson shook his head. "I have no idea."

John jumped in. "I'm just here until they get the paperwork sorted out."

Hector looked even more confused. He slowly sat back down. "Sure."

Mr. Henderson indicated the empty space beside Hector's desk. "We'll put you here," he said to John.

He saw Janice the Janitor coming from the hall leading to the lobby and continuing toward the hall that led to *'you know'*. She had a push broom in hand. She was carrying it, not using it.

Janice was in her early thirties, attractive, dressed in clean coveralls. Her long hair was pulled back into a ponytail; her makeup was enough to do the job without anything extra.

"Janice!" Mr. Henderson called out. "I need you to bring this man a desk."

"I clean the station," said Janice, not stopping. "I don't furnish it."

"Then find Troy," growled Mr. Henderson.

Janice continued across the way, and the others could just make out the words: *yes, sir. Certainly, sir.*

With that, Mr. Henderson looked around the room as if evaluating to ensure the situation was well in hand. Satisfied, he started back toward his office.

"Take him under your wing, Hector," he said, then to John: "Welcome aboard, John Smith."

John watched the station manager return to his office, then turned to look down at Hector.

Hector grinned at the new arrival. "Hey," he said.

John looked up from Hector and glanced around the room. He saw the big "KHDZ" sign that hung on one wall.

"A television station?"

"We develop all our own shows, right from here."

"But... that's crazy. Isn't it?"

"The owner would disagree." Hector indicated a large, heavy plank door directly below the 'KHDZ' sign. "Mr. Horn," he said.

John looked apprehensively toward the door. A small plaque read 'private'.

"KHDZ," said Hector, leaning back in his chair again. "Serving Hades and outlying suburbs. Broadcasting local programming 24 hours a day."

"So I heard," said John.

"Welcome to the organization. Make yourself comfy."

"I'm not going to be around long enough to get comfy. As soon as the paperwork gets straightened out, I'm gone." John pointed heavenward. "Ya know?"

"Sure." Hector turned his attention to Miss Constance, who was approaching from the direction of the program sets.

Miss Constance was a tall, attractive, middle-aged woman who used makeup and attire in an attempt to not look middle-aged.

"A new face," she said cheerily.

Hector remained sitting, but spoke formally. "Miss Constance. Meet John Smith, recently arrived from topside."

John reached out and shook hands with Miss Constance. "Just here temporarily," he stated quickly. "Until the paperwork gets straightened out."

"Of course, dear," she answered coolly.

"Miss Constance is the hostess of 'Up All Night with Miss Constance'," said Hector.

"Ah. I see," said John.

"And just what is it that you will be doing here, John Smith?" asked Miss Constance.

"Call me John."

"If you like," she said smoothly, raising a brow.

"I guess I'm going to be the associate producer."

"Is that so?" Miss Constance looked to Hector. "We don't have a producer, do we Hector?"

Hector shook his head calmly from side to side and Miss Constance turned her attention back to John.

"We don't have a producer, John," said Miss Constance. "We only have our station manager. In order for there to be an associate producer, I would think that we would first need a producer."

"I don't know. I suppose," said John. "I mean, that makes sense."

"Come to think of it, I should think my program would have its own producer. Yes?"

John looked as though he had been cornered. "I guess so."

Miss Constance smiled sweetly. "How would you like to be my producer, John?"

"I don't know."

"Come, come dear. A promotion. And this being your first day."

"Well, I—"

"Enough said." Miss Constance turned away dismissively and started toward Mr. Henderson's office.

"Yes," said Hector, a quiet calm. "That would be Miss Constance."

Chapter 2

John and Hector stood before a television monitor mounted on a wall in the station floor. Behind them, Mike Johansen stepped around the desk and came up beside them.

"Mr. Smith," he said with a nod. He was a well-groomed man in his early sixties, with a smooth, polished look. Mike was the host of "*Good Morning with Mike Johansen*".

"Mr. Johansen," said John. "I caught part of your show this morning. Interesting."

"Thank you." Mike's attention was focused on the television. "Did I miss it?"

"Jim just asked him the final question," said Hector without looking away from the monitor.

Jim, host of "*The Hot Seat*", had an excited, happy voice no matter what the circumstance. "Oh... I'm sorry, Bob. That's wrong," he said cheerily. "You know what that means... *that's right*... it's time for..."

The unseen audience joined in for Jim's finale: "... *the Hot Seat!*"

This was immediately followed by Bob's horrifying scream: "Ahhhhh!!!"

John, Hector and Mike Johansen all grimaced. For Hector and Mike it appeared more playful than genuine.

"That's all for today, folks," Jim said cheerily. "Join us next time, when Bob once again takes—"

The unseen audience again joined in with a roaring cheer: "... *the Hot Seat!!!*"

John, Hector and Mike turned away from the television monitor. John looked horrified.

"What kind of sadistic game show was that?"

"Hector spoke matter-of-factly. "The Hot Seat," he said. He stepped around behind his desk and sat down.

"What'd you expect, son?" asked Mike.

"I didn't expect any of this." John pointed accusingly at the monitor. "But that…"

"Yes." Mike grimaced and grinned at the same time. "Poor ole Bob."

"Every day?" asked John.

"Every day," said Mike.

"Until he wins," Hector sighed.

"Then what?"

Mike sat on the edge of Hector's desk and shrugged a shoulder. "Then they invite some other poor shmuck from down the hall."

John's gaze kept returning to the television monitor, now turned off. "How long as Bob been… *losing*?"

"Oh, must be what?" Mike looked thoughtfully over at Hector.

"About a year." Hector shrugged. "A little more."

"It'll be a sad day around here when Bob leaves," said Mike, standing. He made ready to get about his business. "He's been a ratings bonanza."

John watched in disbelief as Mike Johansen strolled away, heading in the direction of the wall of sets, finally disappearing around a corner.

"I can see why he's here," said John.

Hector smiled an understanding smile. "Mike's not so bad," he said. "And he puts on a heck of a good program."

"Yes. I saw." He said mocking, "I'm Mike Johansen, and you're watching '*Good Morning with Mike Johansen*'."

"That's pretty good," said Hector. "Don't let Mike catch you doing that. He's got a copyright on it and it's fully registered with the head office."

A desk suddenly appeared from the passageway. The tiny figure of Troy was hunched behind it, pushing it noisily across the floor. He maneuvered it around the other furniture and slid it into position beside Hector's desk.

He grinned a satisfied, gnome-like grin. "One desk, as requested."

John placed the fingertips of one hand hesitantly on the top of the desk, as if not ready to accept what this meant, not ready to acknowledge that he now had a place here.

He gave a silent thank you nod. Troy proudly strutted off.

Hector waited just long enough for Troy to disappear around the corner before commented. He turned slowly about in his chair, spoke in a calm statement.

"That desk works better with a chair, John."

There was a golden glow to the tunnel that came from unseen lighting. John walked down the center of the hallway, occasionally glancing down at a small piece of paper with his room number scribbled on it.

He stopped at '63C' and stuffed the paper into his jacket pocket. He pulled out an ornate key and unlocked the door.

His cell was a small, high-ceilinged cave. A faded area rug covered the center of the floor. There was a bed, a desk and chair, and a dresser. Another door opened to an empty closet, and an open archway led to a small bathroom.

John was surprised to see a closed curtain on the far wall. Behind the curtain, however, he found only more rock. He let it fall back into position and wandered over to the bed. He set down with a heavy plop.

"It could be worse," he mumbled. "Not much. But worse."

Mike Johansen sat in one of two comfortable easy chairs on the set of his program 'Good Morning with Mike Johansen'. The Mayor of Hades sat in the other chair, a large coffee cup in hand. He was an older, overstuffed gentleman. He had a pleasant appearance about him. He looked very comfortable on the set, very familiar with the surroundings.

Behind them was a red stone wall. Hanging on the wall was a sign that read 'Good Morning with Mike Johansen'. To one side of the set was the entrance to a dark tunnel leading to back stage.

As with all the KHDZ programming, there were no cameras visible.

"We're back," said Mike Johansen, "and we're talking with the Mayor about plans for the upcoming celebrations. Mr. Mayor, before the break you were hinting that your office has few new events in the works. Care to elaborate?"

"And spoil the surprise?" The Mayor grinned playfully. "You know me better than that, Mike. Let me just say that we're doing our best to make this the finest Founder's Day ever."

"You're setting the bar awfully high, Mr. Mayor. I've been through a few real gems in my time."

"And I've been personally involved in the planning of two hundred and ninety six of them."

"Has it really been that long?" asked Mike. "I can hardly believe it."

"It's true. It's true. In four months, I'll have served this community as its mayor for two hundred and ninety six years."

There was the sound of light applause in the background.

"And you've served us so very well, Mr. Mayor," said Mike Johansen.

More light applause.

"I appreciate your kind words," said the Mayor.

"Well deserved, sir." Mike shifted position and put on an investigative look. "Can you tell us who we might expect to see standing at the speaker's podium this year?"

"I know what you're asking, Mike," said the Mayor, slowly shaking his head from side to side, "and I'm afraid I can't give you a definite 'yes' on that. I don't know whether or not he'll make it back in time. What I am certain of is that he will try."

"So, you haven't spoken with him, then?"

"I wouldn't know how to contact him. Would you?"

At that, there was more light, gentle laughter in the background.

Mike Johansen grinned slyly. "I'll get my staff right on it." Once the follow-up laughter had faded, Mike's smile also faded. "Seriously, though... he has been away quite a long time."

"To our loss, Mr. Horn has been unable to attend the last two of our Founder's Day celebrations."

"And we all know how much he enjoys them," said Mike, smiling genuinely.

"Perhaps this year, Mike. I certainly hope so."

John came into the station floor. He saw Hector sitting at his desk, watching the conclusion to Mike's *Good Morning* show on the monitor. He was calm and quiet, and seemed to be enjoying the program.

John heard Mike Johansen's voice coming over the speakers.

"You unquestionably speak for us all, Mr. Mayor," said Mike. "Well sir, it has been absolutely great talking with you, and I hope you'll come back to visit us again real soon."

"I certainly will, Mike," came the voice of the Mayor. "Thank you so much for having me."

Mike's tone changed as he turned his attention to the viewers. "Next up, we're going to taking a closer look at the *Bob* phenomenon. Bob is a favorite of KHDZ viewers, and of the staff here at the station. What is it about this exceptional individual that keeps us tuning in day after day? What makes Bob so hot? What makes Bob *sizzle*?"

There was pause for effect, then Mike spoke more formally. "We're back in sixty seconds."

The KHDZ blurb kicked in. The announcer's voice was a cross between Darth Vader and a BBC news anchor. "This is KHDZ, <u>the</u> source for news and entertainment, serving Hades and surrounding suburbs."

A twangy, irritating commercial jingle started up and John decided that he more important things to do. He left Hector and walked to the hallway that led to the front lobby.

The lobby was long and narrow. Entering from the station floor, the only other door was set into the wall opposite, glass double-doors with a sign above it that read "Not an Exit".

Emily the Receptionist sat behind the counter facing the glass doors. She was a young woman with the constant look of boredom about her.

"Good morning, Emily," said John. "Anything come in for me this morning?"

Emily spoke flatly, exuding an air of indifference. "No."

"Has anything come in for Mr. Henderson about me?"

"No."

"Would you have told me if anything had in fact come in for Mr. Henderson about me?"

She gave a bored shrug. "Why not..."

"But it's been three days."

"I've been here two hundred years," Emily droned. "I've never gotten anything."

"But... I'm *expecting* this. As soon as the paperwork is cleared up—"

"Uh huh."

John Smith and Emily the Receptionist stared at each other in silence for several seconds. Emily's was blank. John's expression was tinged with anxiety.

He finally turned away from the counter in frustration.

"Thank you, Emily."

"Uh huh..."

Mr. Henderson was working at his desk when he heard a knock on his door.

"Come in," he said.

John entered the station manager's office and closed the door delicately behind him.

"Good morning, Mr. Henderson. Can I speak with you?"

Mr. Henderson glanced up from his paperwork. "I understand you've been annoying Emily."

"Uh..." Geez, that was fast.

Mr. Henderson leaned back in his chair. There was a hint of frustration in the manager's tired expression.

"John Smith. *Sir*. The bureaucracy in which you find yourself, in the very best of circumstances, is excruciatingly slow. The simplest of requests can take decades to see resolution. Now then... Sir... we come to your particular dilemma, for which there is no precedent. There is no process in place in which to resolve such a situation."

"But—"

"How long have you been here?"

"Three days."

"Three days." Mr. Henderson groaned a tired sigh. "Mr. Smith, it takes the bureaucracy of which I speak ten times three days to pass gas. It may be a thousand times three days before your situation rises to the top of some low-level administrator's overstuffed in-box. It may be a thousand times that before it arrives at the desk of someone who has even the slightest inkling of where your situation should actually be directed."

He leaned forward across his desk. "Shall I go on?"

"But sir—"

"I shall go on. At that point in the journey, your situation will have as yet even to be looked at. Still, we might choose to call it progress, as it will have by then at least made its way into the bureaucratic machine."

"Yes sir."

Mr. Henderson's gaze had just the faintest hint of empathy, but was mixed with impatience.

"You are going to be here while."

"Yes sir."

"Consider yourself fortunate that someone in this bureaucracy that we deride thought to put you here at the station to await resolution."

Mr. Henderson positioned himself over his paperwork, spoke one last comment as he returned to his work. "Reflect on the alternative; that you could instead be spending a few thousand years—"

"Yes. I know. Down the hall."

"Exactly. Down the hall."

John watched downcast as Mr. Henderson shuffled through files. The conversation was ended. The meeting was over.

John stood outside the manager's office, his back to the door. His shoulders sagged and he had a dejected look on his face.

He heard a woman's voice.

"Well that's just pathetic."

John looked up. Janice stood beneath the KHDZ sign, leaning on her broom. As ever, she was dressed in clean coveralls.

"Excuse me?" asked John.

"I don't think I've ever seen anyone come out of Henderson's office looking quite so pitiful. Did he eat your children?"

John didn't look as though he was going to respond to Janice's sarcasm, but finally put on as brave a face as was possible given the circumstances. "He clarified a few things for me," he said. "Thank you for your interest. Janice, is it?"

Janice gave a slight nod of the head and pushed off her broom, taking a step nearer to John. "Split a bagel?"

"What?"

"Not one of those rocks you get in the mess hall. I know a cave a few levels down that makes the greatest bagels ever." She planted her broom once again and leaned on it. "A quiet little café. Nice place to sort out any issues that might be bouncing around in your head."

"Sure," John said finally, stumbling for something, *anything*, a little wittier. But he had nothing. "Why not?"

They started toward the passageway. Janice spoke matter-of-fact as they walked.

"He's been known to do that, you know."

"Do what?"

"Eat children."

John and Janice sat at one of five small tables in the café, two coffee mugs and two halves of a bagel on the tabletop between them. One side of the little shop was open to the tunnel. Only one of the other tables was occupied; a man reading a newspaper. The paper was yellow.

The barista, a tall young woman with numerous piercings, stood behind the counter, appearing bored.

"I didn't know there were places like this," said John. "You know... in here, I mean."

"A café here and there, a deli or two, couple of shops." Janice lifted a brow and lowered her head conspiratorially. "Not officially, mind you. This is still a company town, after all; not really supposed to frequent non-sanctioned establishments. But then, if we had followed the rules, none of us would be here, would we? Present company excepted."

"Thanks." He pulled a piece of bagel off his half, put it in his mouth and chewed. "I still..." he fumbled for words. "A television station?"

"So you're okay with the idea of Hades, and that we're walking around in the afterlife, such as it is, but the concept of a television station somehow has you flummoxed?"

"No," he blurted, too quickly. "Yes... No, I'm not okay with any of this. None of it makes any sense."

"Haven't quite reached the acceptance stage," she stated knowingly.

John grew introspective. "Maybe I'm in a hospital," he thought aloud. "Back in the real world. I'm in mental limbo between life and death, and none of this is really happening."

"Speaking just for myself now, John, I can't say as I like that idea very much."

John Smith took another long sip of his coffee, glanced at the barista, at the man reading the newspaper, then out into the tunnel.

"Yeah, well, if I ever come out of it, I'll do my best to bring you out with me."

"Thanks. I'd appreciate that."

Chapter 3

John and Janice were still sitting at the small table. The bagel was gone, the coffee cups near empty. Behind the counter, the barista was resting her chin in an upturned palm.

The man reading the newspaper reservedly turned the page, folded the newspaper back and continued reading.

No one else had come into the café.

"If it wasn't so awful for you, it would be funny," said Janice. "I've been here over a hundred years... a hundred and twelve, actually... and I've never heard of such a thing."

"That's what Mr. Henderson said," grumbled John.

"He'd know. He's been around a lot longer than me."

"Just how long 'we talking, here?"

"Gotta be five, six hundred years, at least. He helped set up the station. That's been... sixty years?"

"And you've been here..." John shifted uncomfortably. "Janice, what did, uh—"

Janice quickly held up a silencing hand.

"Couple of unspoken rules here, John. Call it Hades etiquette. First, don't ask what brought someone down here. The reasons are usually messy; well, except for yours. Which is mildly amusing. But, you understand."

"Sure." *No I don't...*

"And some of us really are trying, each in our own small way, to make up for what we did topside."

"I understand."

Janice stared down at the remnants of her bagel, nodded slowly. "Well, even if you don't now, you will before too long."

"No, really. I get it."

"Good... good." She smiled thinly. "Second rule, guideline really, but strongly encouraged. We don't usually talk about what things were like up there at the time of our... *relocation*."

"Okay... why?"

"You see, we all come here from very different times. The world was very different when I left it than when you left it."

"Sure, but why don't you want to know what's new up there?"

Janice took a moment, finally shrugged on shoulder. "We see enough. You can tell a lot, observing people when they come in."

"But there have been so many changes."

"I know that. Hey, the very existence of the television station. But... we're here. Forever. Really, what's the point?"

John studied the face across the table from him. At first he thought he might have an answer her question, but in the end he held his silence.

The "Debbie's Kitchen" program set consisted of a high stone counter and a massive stone hearth set into the back wall of rough-hewn rock.

Debbie stood behind the stone counter, the hearth rising up behind her. She looked like she was in her twenties, but of course appearances were very misleading.

She was petite, had a child-like face, brown hair with bangs. She had a bubbly personality.

"Hello, everybody! Welcome to Debbie's Kitchen. I'm Debbie. Do I have a great show for you! I sure do."

She leaned against the counter and smiled. "Today we're going to shine the bright Debbie Light on a problem we've all had to face again and again and again." She gave an exaggerated knowing nod. "Some of you may already have guessed what I'm talking about, yes?"

Debbie paused for a calculated two seconds, "I'm speaking of the historic dilemma of ten hot dogs and eight buns. Uh-huh! You set out to prepare a nice meal, and if you're like me, you want everything organized just so..." As she talked, Debbie simulated the actions that she was describing. "You place your package of hot dogs on the counter. You place your package of buns right beside your hot dogs. You open the hot dogs, you open the buns, and what do you find?"

Debbie looked as if she was expecting an answer from the unseen television audience.

"Ten hot dogs, eight buns." Heavy disappointment. "I mean, really... what do you do now?

Another two seconds of calculated pause, and Debbie perked up, straightened up, and put on a big Debbie grin.

"Well, I have the answer! When we return, I'm going to show you what to do with those two extra wieners. Stay right where you are! I'll be right back!"

Out on the station floor, John and Janice stood in front of the television monitor mounted high on the wall. Behind them, Hector sat at his desk, diligently going about his work.

John had a slightly stupefied look on his face, while Janice looked somewhat bored. To her, it was all quite familiar.

"That's Debbie," she said, in a flat, unemotional tone.

"Yes," John said numbly.

"I don't think she's all there."

"No." They turned away from the monitor, started across the station floor. On the far side of the floor, Debbie's set was visible. "It's all a joke though, right?"

They passed by Hector, who spoke without looking up from his work. "Remember where you are," he said dryly.

"Not many people care one way or the other about her show. Even if they did, no one is going to say anything."

They stopped in front of Mr. Henderson's office. Janice leaned close to John. "Rumor is that Debbie is Mr. Horn's daughter."

John turned his head sharply in the direction of the heavy wooden door to the office of the opposite wall. He looked then across the room, to the opposite wall. Debbie was standing behind her kitchen counter holding a limp hot dog in one hand.

He turned back to Janice. "You're kidding."

Janice shrugged noncommittally. "That was the rumor going around when the station started up."

John looked again across the cavernous room. Debbie was waving the hot dog above her head.

John came out of the station manager's office a few minutes later and wandered over to his desk.

Hector was sitting on the edge of his own desk, arms folded, eyes glued to the television monitor. John stood beside him, curious to see what had Hector so enthralled.

Hector was watching the soap opera "Moments of Our Nonexistence".

Bill and Joan were on the screen...

"Bill... oh, Bill..." said Joan tearfully, dramatically.

"Joan, Joan..." said Bill, just as dramatic.

"Oh, Bill..."

"Joan... why do you turn from me?" Long pause. "Joan?"

"You know why, Bill! You know why!"

The program cut dramatically to the soap opera's blurb, spoken smoothly and eloquently by the show's unseen narrator:

"Like lava through the flume, so flow the mindless Moments of Our Nonexistence."

Hector used the remote to mute the television, stood and returned to his chair behind his desk. He sat, a satisfied look spreading across his face.

"Hey, John," he said, almost as if noticing John for the first time. "So, what did Mr. Henderson have to say? Is he finally puttin' you to work?"

John dropped down into his own chair. He leaned over his desk, his expression much more somber than Hector's.

"That depends very much on your definition of the word work."

"Yeah," said Hector, a faint smile spreading across his face. "Miss Constance gettin' what she wants, is she?"

"He was glad to have something to me to assign me to."

"Yeah, well... *temporary*, right?"

John ignored the sarcasm, with some difficulty.

"The extent of my duties," he began. "Come up with a crappy movie for Miss Constance to '*offer up to her audience*' each night, see to it that she has strawberries or cherries or grapes or something to munch seductively on while she 'heavy breathes' to said audience... and, finally, see that she has an appropriately alluring night garment to wear each night as she lounges upon her purple couch."

"Sounds like an associate producer to me," said Hector.

"Really?"

"Come on man. Hell if I know." Hector began sorting through papers on his desk. "At least I don't have to do it anymore."

Chapter 4

John stepped through the narrow archway from his bathroom into the main room of his small quarters. He was dressed in pants and no shirt, had a bath towel over one shoulder and his hair was wet. A hint of warm moisture hung in the air.

He stopped short at the sight of Troy lounging comfortably across the bed, resting on one elbow.

"What the—"

"Good morning, John Smith!" Troy said, as pleasant as could be.

"Troy, what are you doing in my room?"

Troy pointed to a sport jacket that was draped over the back of the only chair.

"Miss Constance asked me to bring that to you," he said, then winked slyly. "She wants her producer to look snazzy..."

"Yeah? That doesn't really answer my question, though, does it?"

Troy sat up. "I don't know what you mean."

"You can't just come into my room," John said sharply.

Troy looked truly perplexed. "Why not?"

Which truly startled John Smith. "Because I said so."

"Really?"

"Yes. Really."

"You don't like me?"

"That's not the point." John pointed at the door. "You knock on the door. If I'm here, I'll open it. If I do open it, I'll ask you in."

Troy thought about that for a moment, intently and very seriously.

"I see," he said at last. "Seems an odd way to go about it, if you ask me."

"I'm not asking you."

Troy slid to the edge of the bed and slowly stood. He gave John a genuinely hurt look, lowered his head and started toward the door.

"Troy..." John sighed loudly. "Troy, I'm sorry. It's just..."

Troy gave a half-glance back to John, but continued his slow, plodding march to the door.

John tried again. "Listen, I have a thing about my space, and this room is my space. That's important to me. All right?"

Troy reached the door. He hadn't yet recovered from the hurt. "Sure, John Smith." He gave a nod to the sport jacket. "I'd wear that, if I were you. You hurt Miss Constance' feelings, you'll regret it. Know what I mean?"

"Sure," John said cautiously.

Troy opened the door, took one step through the threshold and stopped. He poked his head back into the room.

"I hear you're spending time with Janice," he said soberly.

"Is that a problem?" asked John, back on defense.

"No." Troy managed a half-smile. "No, I suppose not. But you might want to stay on your toes with that one."

"Why?"

"I like you, John Smith." Troy shrugged his pointed shoulders. "I wouldn't want to see you get hurt."

"That's ridiculous."

"Just sayin'."

John watched the door close. He looked over at the sport jacket that was so carefully draped over the back of the chair.

After a quick glance at the door to make sure that Troy wasn't going to unexpectedly return, he stepped over to the chair and lifted up the jacket.

It wasn't bad... not gaudy, not too flashy, not too conservative. A bit of quality and class with just a hint of restraint.

Hector came out of Mr. Henderson's office, walked over to his desk and sat down. Across from him sat John Smith, dressed in a nice sport jacket, a stack of DVDs on his desk. John absently set another atop the stack.

"Picked one out for tonight?" he asked John.

John spoke wearily. "Thought I'd go with 'Vampires from Bikini Island'."

Hector smiled approvingly. "Oh, I may just have to stay up for that one."

"Don't toy with me, Hector."

"Come on, John... you gotta learn to get into your work. You have to do whatever it takes to keep the job fun and interesting."

"You say so..."

"Hey. Look around. You're here. Who knows for how long? Years at least. Could be centuries. Could be—" he gave a questioning shrug of the shoulders. "Ya' know? Might as well make the best of it."

"Peachy." John looked warily at the stack of DVDs on his desk.

Troy appeared on the station floor, coming in from the hallway, continued on the walkway. He looked a bit agitated. He stopped midway to the opposite hall, near the massive wooden door to Mr. Horn's office.

He looked into the center of the station, tilted his head slightly as he considered Hector and John. He smiled then, visibly relaxed, raised a hand and waved.

Hector and John both waved back. John's wave was cautious and uncertain, while Hector's was casual.

Troy lowered his hand and turned his sharply in the direction of the main hallway from where he had just come. He frowned, turned and stalked out of the room, disappearing back into the hallway.

Hector had already turned his attention to the papers on his desk.

John, however, was carefully eyeing the threshold through which Troy had just passed.

"Hector..." questioningly.

"Yeah..." absently.

"What is it with Troy?"

Hector grinned but continued digging through his paperwork. "He is an odd one, isn't he?"

"I found him in my room this morning," said John.

"Yeah?" Hector leaned back in his chair, tossed a folder aside. "Yeah?" He didn't seem surprised.

"I came out of the shower, and he's laying there on my bed."

"That would be Troy," said Hector, nodding. "I once found him actually in my shower. He's got access to just about everywhere; here and down the hall."

"He can go anywhere he wants? Just walk in and put his feet up?"

"Pretty much." It didn't seem to bother him.

"But..." John fumbled for a word, frustrated. "How?"

Hector said nothing. He waited for John to come up with the reason.

John glanced in the direction of Mr. Horn's heavy wooden door. "Is it true that he's, you know... He and ..."

"Connected?" Hector slowly sat forward, placed his arms on the desk in front of him. "Troy has been around as long as anyone can remember. Before the station. Back when we were—" His face darkened faintly, as if shadowed from a memory. "Mr. Horn brought Troy up with him when we were first getting this place set up."

"And they're related..." John stated.

"That's what people say." Hector shrugged. "Cousins or something. Whatever substitutes for that down here."

Seems to be a lot of that, thought John. He was dully bewildered. "Troy is annoying, but I haven't seen anything that would make him... like... you know..."

"Hey, man, we all got it in us." Hector managed another very faint smile. "I mean, we're here, right?"

"Right," John frowned. "I think I'll sleep with one eye open."

"I do."

The '*Tell it to Judge Roy*' set was a small, high-ceilinged cavern. Dominating the room was the judge's reddish brown stone bench. It towered over the plaintiff's rickety wooden witness podium.

There was a small raised platform to one side of the judge's bench where the silent, ever-present bailiff stood. On the opposite side was a small wooden table at which sat the also silent, also ever-present recorder.

Judge Roy, moderator for the *Tell it to Judge Roy* program, sat high up on his stone bench. He appeared to be in his sixties, but had the look about him that implied he had led a wild, maybe even dangerous life.

He looked coolly down on Edward, today's first plaintiff, who stood nervously at the plaintiff's podium.

Edward was a nondescript middle-aged man who had the anxious look of someone who has recently come to realize that just maybe it had been a mistake to have volunteered to appear on the Judge Roy program.

The unseen narrator spoke the program's blurb in a voice deep and serious.

"You think you've been wronged?

"You think you've been screwed?

"Well stop you're whining, Citizen.

"You know what ya gotta do...

"That's right..."

The studio audience joined in with the last line:

"Tell it to Judge Roy!"

This was followed by the sound of applause from the unseen audience.

The narrator waited for the applause to end.

"We'll be right back to introduce our first plaintiff."

This was followed by the sound of an annoying commercial jingle. All the while, the camera remained focused on the nervous Edward.

The commercial jingle ended.

"We're back," the narrator said somberly.

More light applause from the unseen audience.

"Meet Edward," said the narrator. "Edward thinks he's been screwed by the system... Let's listen in."

"All right, Edward," said Judge Roy from high above the plaintiff. "Let me hear it."

As he listened, Judge Roy silently read through the pile of paperwork concerning Edward's case.

"Yes, sir," said Edward. "I filed an appeal concerning my case some time back, and I have every reason to believe the appeal was denied for reasons of prejudice. Sir."

"Appeal..." Judge Roy said absently, again without looking at Edward.

"Yes, sir. I appealed my uh... the decision that... that placed me here rather than up, uh—"

"I get it," Judge Roy said impatiently.

"Judge Roy, I don't think they looked at the appeal at all. They didn't consider how I had turned things around. I believe they were prejudiced by the... circumstances... of the *incident*, and never looked beyond that."

The judge nodded several times and finally looked up from the paperwork. He spoke very precisely.

"Two points of order here, sailor. Both of 'em are biggies," he began. "An incident such as yours is what <u>gets</u> people sent here. It is the <u>reason</u> for this place. Using it as an argument against the decision to send you here isn't likely to help your case. Second, the decision to send you here wasn't made here. It was made upstairs. And you know this."

Judge Roy held up a pile of papers. "This is isn't your first appeal. You've filed three, going back eight hundred years. Two of them upstairs. They were both summarily tossed out. You filed a third downstairs, knowing full well they had no jurisdiction."

Judge Roy carefully placed the papers back onto the stack in front of him. "You waste my time, Edward. The determination made regarding your situation is no more within my purview than that of anyone else down here. You knew that coming before me."

"No, sir!" cried Edward. "I swear I—"

"And now you would mock my intelligence."

"I'm sorry, sir. I never—"

"I find you to be a thoroughly offensive individual."

Edward started to protest yet again, but wisely decided against it.

Judge Roy leaned back until he was barely visible to the plaintiff standing at the podium below him. He came to a decision, let out a long, noisy sigh.

"Unfortunately, in and of itself, being offensive isn't a crime. However, I _can_ hold you to account for the knowing and wanton consumption of the time that my staff and I have expended on your behalf." He lifted and dropped his gavel. "So be it."

Edward looked shocked and dismayed. "But I came to you for help! I came to you for help!"

Judge Roy had already dismissed this abuser of his time. He calmly set Edward's files aside and reached down to take a new set that was being silently offered to him by his bailiff.

"Next case," he said.

At that, two large, burly guards came into the room and stood to either side of Edward. He looked fearfully at one and then the other, then turned frantically to Judge Roy.

"Judge Roy!" he cried desperately. "Judge Roy, No!"

Judge Roy opened the file of the next plaintiff and began reviewing the case.

The two guards reached calmly for Edward.

"And we'll be right back..." said the narrator.

John came out of his room and closed the door. He took one step, then quickly reached back to make certain the door was locked. Satisfied, he started down the long hallway.

After four or five steps, he began to hear nightmarish sounds coming from behind him, coming from...

..._down the hall._

He slowed his step, finally stopped.

He turned and listened.

Cries of anguish... coming from somewhere beyond the bend in the hall.

He started toward the sounds. He took a step, and another.

He stood in a darkened hallway. There was a flickering red glow beyond another bend in the tunnel ahead of him.

Empty, echoing hollow sounds...

Troy stepped up beside him.

"What is that?" asked John.

"It is whatever you imagine to be."

Neither said anything more for several moments.

"I don't belong here," John said at last.

"It was a mistake that brought you here, John Smith, but this is where you need to be."

"Why?"

"You must be here."

A long pause... a long, tired sigh.

"I had a life. It wasn't great, but it had meaning. It had purpose. This... this is..."

"It is necessary," Troy said smoothly. "You must be here."

"Must be? Must be? I'm not supposed to be here at all."

There was another long pause. John's expression slowly faded to inevitable surrender.

"How long? When can I go—" John hesitantly pointed heavenward. "Up?"

"I do not know."

"Ever?"

"Yes, John Smith," said Troy confidently. "One day."

When John got to the café, Janice was waiting, sitting at the same table where the two of them had sat before. The only other person in the café was the barista, who was quietly going about her business behind the counter.

John had a studious look on his face as he sat down opposite Janice. He could see that the coffee mug on the table in front of her was half empty.

Janice glanced up. "You wear your emotions, John."

"Do I?"

"You do. What's up?"

"Interesting phrase."

"What?"

"Nothing."

"Sure." Janice shrugged one shoulder.

John again groped for words. "Janice... do you ever go down the hall?"

Janice had appeared prepared for whatever John might say, but this was unexpected. It takes her a moment or two to respond.

"Now and then," she said finally. "My job."

She turned her coffee mug absently, picked it up, set it carefully back down. "I spent some time there myself, you know; before the station opened."

John said nothing. He hadn't thought about that. There were a few moments of uncomfortable silence.

He looked over at the barista and managed to get her attention without calling out to her. He indicated that would like the same as whatever Janice was drinking. The barista nodded silently and set about preparing John's order.

John turned his attention back to Janice.

"I'm hearing a lot more..." he decided not to specify what it was that he was hearing a lot more of. "From down there. Lately."

"Yes, I suppose you would," she said flatly. "Founder's Day coming up soon."

"What?"

"Founder's Day. They're getting ready."

"What does—"

"Some of the activities... they're practicing."

John looked unsettled. "I see."

He of course did not see. He was glad when the barista brought his mug and set it down on the table. It was a welcome distraction from his thoughts.

"Oh, I almost forgot," he said. "I submitted my name to Judge Roy."

"You did what?

"Judge Roy. I put my name in."

"Withdraw it."

"What? Why? They said I have a good chance of getting on the show. They've heard of me."

"Of course they've heard of you. They've heard of everybody. You go down there and you pull your name out."

John couldn't understand why this had Janice so upset.

"Why should I?" He leaned across the table. "I don't plan to spend the next thousand years down here waiting for some bureaucrat to put my paperwork in the right in-box."

"This won't help. They're not about winning, John. They're about ratings."

"And you don't think my getting outta here won't make ratings?"

"Don't be an idiot. They ain't got that kinda' pull. Nobody down here has that kinda' pull."

John stared down at his coffee. "One way or another, Janice. I'm getting out of here."

"What? You gonna escape?" She sounded incredulous. "From Hell? From what I've been able to observe in my limited time down here, the place is pretty much escape proof."

John's expression turned slowly from defiance to crestfallen. He slumped back in his chair. "I can't just sit back and wait."

"I'm really, really sorry, John." Janice's words were softer now. "I'm telling you. There's one way in, and there ain't no out. And Judge Roy... he'll burn ya'."

Chapter 5

It was late at night and the station floor lights were turned down low. The only significant lighting came from the Up All Night program set.

John stood in the shadows, watching Miss Constance. She was lounging on the purple couch that was the centerpiece of her set. She wore a long, flowing nightgown that showed everything while showing absolutely nothing.

She munched playfully on purple grapes.

Hector came up from behind John, rested a hand on his shoulder.

"Not bad, John," he said.

"Thanks."

"One thing, though. I wouldn't go grapes with vampires."

"You wouldn't."

"No. No, I wouldn't," said Hector. "Cherries, I think. Yeah, definitely cherries."

"I'll remember that," John said, half-hearted. "Cherries with vampires."

"Good man."

They watched Miss Constance in silence for few moments.

"What kind of work did you do topside, John?" asked Hector. He continued to watch Miss Constance toy with her unseen audience.

"I thought we weren't supposed to talk about our lives topside?"

"Why not?"

"Janice. She said—"

"Janice told you that?"

"One of the rules, she said. We don't talk about what got us sent here, and or what things were like up there when we left."

"Well that doesn't make much sense. Miss Constance' movies show us what things are like."

"Not so much," John smirked.

"Okay, but you know what I mean," Hector said sheepishly. He watched Miss Constance pop a grape with her teeth. "One of the reasons Mr. Horn likes this show is it lets the citizens see what they're missing."

"I suppose that makes some sadistic sense."

"Exactly," said Hector. He turned his attention from Miss Constance to John. "Janice has a long list of rules; rules for everything. They help her feel she has some control, down here where we have very little."

"She's a purposeful woman."

"Not letting you talk about what you did means that you can't ask her about what she did."

"What did she do?"

"Never heard. See?"

"Troy seems to know something."

"Yeah, well Troy knows something about everything."

On the program set, Miss Constance lifted a seductive shoulder and let out a catlike purr.

Hector nodded in her direction. "A real firecracker, that one," he said. "No one knows what she did either but she was hanged as witch."

"Then she's been here a while."

"I suppose. Mr. Horn brought her up to the station early on. Same with most of us."

Hector admired Miss Constance a moment more, turned to leave.

"Good job with the show," he said.

John watched him take a couple of steps. "Hey, Hector..." he called out softly.

Hector stopped and turned back. "Yeah?"

"This Founder's Day thing... pretty big around here?"

"Nothing bigger."

"Big."

"What else you got down here? You plan, you build, you create... The big day comes, you do your thing, you walk around and see what everyone else is doing."

"Like what?"

"I don't know, man. Booths, games, speeches, the parade." His thin smile was almost sad. "And don't forget the television specials."

"I see what you mean; sounds like a living hell."

Hector looked confused at first, then let out a quiet laugh and smiled broadly.

"Hey, not bad, man. Good to see you getting into the swing of things."

Hector turned about again and took several more steps before John again called out to him, still working to keep his voice low. Hector stopped yet again and turned. This time he waited silently for whatever it was that John wanted now.

"I was a teacher," said John.

It took Hector a few moments to realize that John was answering the question that had started this whole conversation going.

"That a fact?"

"School for troubled kids," said John.

"Good man." Hector stepped into the dark.

John turned his attention back to Miss Constance, who pulled a grape from the bunch with her teeth and drew it seductively into her mouth.

John stood alone and silent in the darkened station, the glow of the Miss Constance program set just reaching his feet, painting his silhouette in half-shadow.

Troy sat alone in one of the chairs in the waiting area outside Mr. Henderson's office, spindly legs crossed, hands clasped and resting on a bony knee.

He gave a slow, casual nod to Hector as he came into the station, passing the waiting area on his way to his desk.

"Good morning, Hector," he said.

"Troy," Hector answered guardedly. He took another couple of steps, stopped and looked back. "Something going on?"

"Not really, no." Troy stared at Mr. Henderson's closed door and frowned. "John Smith is not a very patient man."

"Ah. Right." Hector looked to Mr. Henderson's office. "Right."

Mr. Henderson leaned forward across his desk, fingers tightly intertwined. He refused to look up at John, standing directly in front of him.

"I told you last week, and the week before that. There is absolutely nothing I can do. No paperwork. No request for an audience. Nothing. You are here until you are told not to be here."

"It's not—"

"I don't care that you don't belong here," said Mr. Henderson. "No one cares that you don't belong here. It doesn't matter one damn bit that you don't belong here."

"Maybe Judge Roy..."

Mr. Henderson laughed, leaned back in his chair. "Yeah. You do that."

"Why not?"

"Have you ever actually watched that show?"

"Once or twice," answered John, defensively.

"Really? And have you ever seen anyone come away happy?"

"Well no, but—"

"Oh, right... you're different."

"I am different. I don't—"

"All right, stop. I've had enough." Mr. Henderson shoved himself forward, looked piercingly up at John. "Now you listen and you listen good. It doesn't matter that you were sent down my mistake. It doesn't matter that you were a wonderful person when you lived in the sunshine. You are here now. You died. You went to hell. Welcome, sir. Want cake?"

Troy stood as the station manager's office door opened and John Smith came out.

"Good morning, John Smith."

John gave a tired nod in response as he closed the door slowly behind him.

"John Smith, I—"

John quickly raised a hand, jabbed a shaky finger.

"Don't – you – say it."

"I just—"

"Don't. I don't want to hear it."

John stood there a moment more, hands shaking. He pushed himself away from the waiting area, out of the station.

Hector watched from his desk, his face fraught with empathy. Troy let out a sympathetic sigh.

"He makes it so difficult."

"Yeah," said Hector. "Good thing you're on his side."

"Yes. Fortunate."

John was sitting on the floor of the dark hallway, just before the bend in the tunnel, from beyond which came the haunting, hollow echoing sounds of empty caverns and the occasional cries of suffering souls.

Debbie came down the hall from the direction of the station. She stood somberly before John, her back to the opposite wall. She studied him a few moments, then slid down until she was sitting on the floor directly in front of him.

"Hey," she said flatly, uncharacteristically non-chipper.

"Hey." John glanced across at her. "Debbie? Debbie's Kitchen?"

"Yep," said Debbie. "John? Just here until the paperwork gets sorted out?"

"Yeah," wearily. "That's me."

Debbie leaned forward and held out her hand. "Hello, John. Pleased to meet you."

John looked at the offered hand for a few moments, finally reached out and they shook hands.

"Hello, Debbie," he said impassively.

"I'm surprised we haven't crossed paths sooner. The station's not that big a place."

"I work the night shift these days," said John. "I've seen you around. Interesting show."

"Uh, huh." Debbie gave a slight grin.

"Yeah, well..."

"So what has you moping out here in the hall?" She glanced in the direction of the bend in the tunnel. "At this particular spot?"

"Just wandering. And feeling sorry for myself."

"I see," she nodded. "You do a lot of that?"

"Oh, yeah. Lots. Lots and lots."

"Hmm. I see. And which you figure gives you the most satisfaction, John? The wanderin', or the self-pity?"

John lifted his gaze at that, looked directly at Debbie. Debbie met his gaze head on, waited for an answer.

"I find both to be revealing," he finally said. "And neither particularly satisfactory."

"I would imagine."

John rested a wrist on one knee, pointed a finger in Debbie's direction. "You're not exactly the perky thing you let on, are you?"

Debbie gave a quick half-smile. Again they studied one another. Again Debbie patiently waited.

John looked to his left, down the hall leading the main part of the station. "I've been exploring these tunnels all day, gone into every nook and cranny. And ya' know what I found?"

"Sure," said Debbie. "A few shops, a handful of cafés, and lots of tunnels with lots of doors with room numbers on 'em."

"Yeah. Pretty much."

"And all that wanderin' and self-pity brought you right back here."

John looked carefully at Debbie and furrowed his brow.

"Who the hell are you?"

Debbie took a moment, then climbed to her feet. She held out a hand for John to take.

"C'mon," she said. "I want to show you something."

John looked at the hand, reached out then and let Debbie help him to his feet.

Debbie led John around the bend in the tunnel.

They stepped out onto a ledge overlooking a pit hundreds of feet deep. The bottom glowed orange and red and purple. There were shifting shadows, but nothing definitive. The hollow, empty echoes were louder here, and there were faint whispering sounds, as of a shifting wind.

The only feature on the ledge was a rough-hewn stone bench.

"Ya' feel that?" asked Debbie.

John's face turned a dull gray. "Oh, geez," he mumbled, suddenly overcome.

Debbie took John's elbow and guided him to the bench. They sat, and Debbie laid a comforting hand on his arm. John took a long, shuddering breath.

"What is that?"

"Give it a minute," she stated. "It'll pass."

They sat in silence on the stone bench. Debbie rested her hands in her lap. A minute passed; maybe more.

"Better?" she asked.

John managed a trembling breath. He nodded, took another, longer breath.

"What... what is it?" he asked again.

Debbie settled back, stared down into the pit.

"Hopelessness," she said quietly.

"Oh, man."

Shadows of burnt orange and purple slithered across the walls. A hollow, empty whisper rose up from the pit.

"I see things sometimes," said Debbie. "Hear things. It reaches up to me. Takes hold of me."

"Then why do you come here?"

The expression on her face drifted from internal suffering to a haunted gaze.

"I was there, down there, for so, so long," she said, not much above a whisper. "I'm never going back. Not ever. I would do anything. Anything." A twinge of a smile then, though a bit forced. "Even Debbie's Kitchen."

"You don't like doing the show?"

"Oh, God no. I thought you said you've seen it?"

"Yes." John grinned slightly, briefly. "But I still don't—"

"Coming here... does something. It sets things right in my head."

John looked away, looked forward, in the direction of the pit.

"I think I get it," he said. A long pause, then. "The wiener episode. Particularly good, I thought."

"Thanks." Debbie grinned pleasantly. "We worked hard on that one."

Another long pause...

"So," John started. "You and... you're not, are you?" IT was a statement of fact more than a question.

"No. We're not."

"Then why—"

"I don't know whether you've noticed. He likes his games."

"I'm getting that."

"You wouldn't believe what I've had to deal with, folks looking to get an in with Daddy."

"Well, I'm glad you're not, you know, daughter of Satan."

"Yeah."

"And thanks." John wiggled a finger at their surroundings. "For the tour."

Debbie's face softened. "No problem."

John stood before the doors in the reception lobby, gazing out. There was nothing beyond the glass. Emily watched indifferently from her post behind the counter.

Janice came in from the hall and crossed the lobby, cast a knowing nod at Emily along the way.

"Hello, John." She stood beside him. "Whatcha doin'?"

"I've been thinking," he said thoughtfully. "When I came through these doors, I was so scared."

"Most understandable," she said. "Not anymore?"

"I'd be crazy not to be scared. Let's just say, I'm starting to gain my footing."

"That's good."

"Hmm," grunted John.

Janice looked about; at the room about her, Emily behind them, behind the counter. At the doors, the sign above the doors that read 'Not an Exit'.

"We didn't have this when I came down," she said. "Didn't have the TV station back then."

"Hmm," John said again. He was on his own line of thought. "Did you leave many folks behind when you died?"

"I told you, we don't—"

"Me, I had this on-again, off-again relationship going. Her name's Carol. She's a good person, but... we don't really have much in common." He thought a moment about that. "I don't think it ever would have worked."

Janice didn't say anything. She was actually a bit frightened.

John continued.

"My sister and I are pretty close. She's a teacher, too. Same school." He smiled at some fading memory. "She has a couple of really great kids. Five and six."

In the glass of the doors then... moving images, faint at first, then sharper, clearer, mixing with the reflections of John and Janice.

A birthday party, young children around a table; a boy smiling in front of his cake and candles. A woman in the background, hint of sadness.

"Eddie had a birthday," sighed John. The image began to fade. "Guess he's seven, now."

The long, drawn out silence was heavy. The glass in front of them now showed only their own reflections staring back at them.

"No," said Janice. "I didn't have anyone."

John turned to her. A warm glance, a soft smile. He reached out, took her hand. She accepted it.

It was a warm moment.

"Let's take it elsewhere, people," said Emily.

John came into his room carrying a portable television and set it down on the bed, leaving the door to the hall open. He looked around the room, then went over to the dresser and dragged it across the floor until it was in a better position to place the TV and be able to watch it from the bed.

He took the television then and set it on the top of the dresser, knelt down and was reaching behind it to plug in the power cord when Janice appeared in the open doorway. She stopped one step inside the room and spoke pleasantly.

"Didn't you say something about there being nothing worth watching?"

John finished plugging in the power cord and stood up. He reached around behind the television and began hooking up the cable.

"Still true," he said. "But Miss Constance is insistent. I don't have to be on the floor all night, but she expects her producer to watch her performance."

Janice looked side-glance at the bed, then back at John. There was a sparkle in her eye and a smirk on her face.

"I see."

John positioned the television for viewing from the bed. "I'm surprised to see you here. I seem to remember you saying something about not spending time in private quarters."

"I think it was more along the lines of 'I seem to spend a lot of time alone in my <u>own</u> quarters'. That doesn't preclude the occasional visit to other quarters."

"I see."

Janice hopped onto the bed, slid back until she could sit with her back to the wall. "What are we watching?"

The lights were off, leaving only the flickering glow of the television to illuminate the room, creating shadows that danced from bed to table to dresser and across the rock walls of John's cell.

He and Janice were lying atop the covers of the bed, watching 'Up All Night with Miss Constance' on the television. They were dressed comfortably, John wearing lounge pants and undershirt, Janice dressed in a loose pullover and short-shorts.

Janice's coveralls were on the nearby chair.

"Where did you find this horrible movie?" she asked.

"Same place I find all of 'em," said John. "In a big box labeled 'Really Bad Movies'."

"Maybe you should find the box labeled 'Not So Bad Movies'."

"That probably misses the point of where we are."

"Why, Mr. Smith. I do think you might finally be getting it."

"Is that so?"

At that, Janice gave John a gentle jab in the side, followed by a light, pleasant kiss. This started to lead to something more when...

On the television, the program cut to an intermission and Miss Constance appeared on the screen. She was lounging playfully on her purple couch and began teasing her audience.

"So, what do you think, my sweeties? She is quite the little vixen, is she not?" Miss Constance gave a come-hither look. "I bet you'd like to try a little of that..."

Janice mumbled, "Not really, no..."

"Well, you might just get your wish, my darlings," Miss Constance continued. "In honor of this year's Founder's Day, I'm sending out a special invitation just for you."

She sat up oh-so-slowly and leaned closer to the unseen camera. She spoke in a husky whisper. "How would you like to spend a night with Miss Constance?"

"What?" Janice blurted.

"Not what you think," John said absently.

"That's right, sweetie," said Miss Constance. "You just drop by the Miss Constance booth and slip me a little piece of paper with your name on it. Who knows? You might be the lucky boy that I choose to have snuggle up here beside me, keep me warm through the long, cold night on an upcoming episode of Up All Night With... *me.*"

Miss Constance giggled like a playful kitten.

"You're kidding," groaned Janice.

"She does enjoy her work," said John.

"I'll see you in person this Founder's Day. Come on by."

Miss Constance shifted position and tone of voice. "Are you ready for more of tonight's feature? Mmm, me too. Oh... but before we do, I want to give a *very special* thank you to someone *very special* out there. You know who you are, my sweetie."

She slid back to a lounging position and gave another of her playful giggles. "Now back to *The Spy Wore Heels.*"

Miss Constance winked as the television image slowly faded and returned to the night's movie feature.

"Just what did she mean by that? Someone very special?" demanded Janice.

"That's very, <u>very</u> special."

Janice was not amused. The glare was withering.

"C'mon Janice," said John. "You know Miss Constance. Always teasing, always leaving them wondering."

"This was more than that. I know her."

"What are you saying?"

"You know very well what I'm saying."

"No. I don't."

"If I find out that you and her—"

"Oh, God no."

"Don't bring Him into this." Janice jabbed a finger at John. "You mind what I say."

She slid off the bed, grabbed her coveralls off the chair. John looked pleadingly after her as she walked toward the bathroom.

"Janice..."

Janice disappeared into the bathroom. If there had been a door to slam, it would have slammed.

John watched the empty threshold for several moments before looking back at the television. A young, leather-clad woman was kicking the bejeezus out of two hapless foes.

"Damn," John grumbled under his breath.

Miss Constance stepped down from her set. She pulled on a less revealing, quite sophisticated housecoat as she approached a small table with two chairs. A serving tray on the table held a small pitcher, several glasses and a dish of cookies.

Judge Roy waited in one of the chairs, watched admiring as Miss Constance sat in the other.

"Good job with the show tonight, Miss Constance."

"Thank you, Roy." Miss Constance poured herself as glass of juice. "What has you up and about so early? You're not much of a morning person, as I recall."

"Bit of trouble sleeping."

"Well, that's not like you at all."

Judge Roy pointed at the pitcher. Miss Constance nodded and waited patiently as the judge poured himself a glass, took a cookie from the dish, and leaned back in his chair.

"How's that producer of yours working out?" he asked.

"Just fine."

"Rather an odd sort, isn't he? This John Smith?"

"How so?"

"I don't know. Bit out of his element, isn't he?" Judge Roy brushed at cookie crumbs on his shirt.

"He's settling in all right." Miss Constance eyed the judge warily. "The wellbeing of my producer has you tossing and turning?"

"Just making conversation." He took a drink of his juice, set the glass down on the table. "I suppose you know he was signed to appear on my show."

"Is that so?"

"All sealed and delivered. Then out of the blue, he's taken out of the lineup. Not a word of explanation."

"Really? That's too bad."

"Yes it is."

"He would have made an interesting plaintiff, I would imagine."

"He certainly would have." Judge Roy finished off the cookie, rubbed the crumbs from his fingers. "You wouldn't have had anything to do with Mr. Smith being pulled, now would you, Connie?"

"What would make you think such a thing?"

"Protecting your boy?" He brushed at crumbs on his shirt. "You've obviously taken a shine to the lad."

"I like him just fine, but what he does in his off hours is no concern of mine."

"Oh come on, Connie. There's nothin' happens 'round here without your blessing."

"Dear Roy, you give me way too much credit. I'm just another tunnel dweller trying to get by."

Judge Roy gave a loud, hearty laugh at that.

"Oh, woman! Would that were so!" He leaned forward, and the missed crumbs rolled onto his lap. "A word from you and the lights don't burn. Shows don't show. Folks I pass in the hall one day, gone the next."

"I believe you're mistaking me for someone else," she said heavily.

"No. No, not at all. I know you. I know you better than anyone knows you."

"That was a very long time ago, Roy."

Judge Roy sat back again. His expression and the sound of his voice went melancholy. "It certainly was, my dear Connie."

He slowly got to his feet. He picked up his glass, took another drink and set it back onto the table.

"You stand so very close to the flame, Miss Constance. If I thought in a million years that you would listen, I would tell you... but then—"

"I'm fine."

"I'm sure you are." He started away, stopped and looked back. "And with young Mr. Smith under your protection, I have no doubt that he is fine, as well."

"As I said," she spoke hesitantly. "You give me too much credit."

"My apologies." Judge Roy nodded politely.

Hector sat at his desk, his full attention to the television mounted on the wall.

Troy was at John's desk, leaning back in the chair, feet up.

"Moments of Our Nonexistence was on. Bill and Joan were in deep, dramatic conversation.

"Joan, Joan..." said Bill. "You can't possibly think that I would ever be with... with... *someone else.*"

"Oh, Bill... Bill," said Joan. "I know all about... her. I know all about... the Other Woman!"

"No, Joan. No!"

"Yes, Bill. I know all about... Alicia!"

"No Joan! No! Joan, don't turn away from me. Please, Joan!"

"I'm sorry, Bill. I'm sorry! I can't bear to look at you. Not knowing... not knowing what I know. Not knowing that..."

"What, Joan?" Bill asked pleadingly. "What is it?"

"I can't... I can't..."

"Tell me, Joan! You must tell me!"

"Alicia is..."

"What are you trying to say, Joan? Please, Joan. Look at me and tell me!"

"Alicia is... Alicia is... *with child!*"

Dramatic closing music, followed by the program narrator, the words spoken smoothly and eloquently... *Like lava through the flume, so flow the mindless Moments of Our Nonexistence.*"

"Why doesn't Joan just kill him and be done with it?" Troy sneered.

Hector clicked the remote in the general direction of the television.

"Because, Troy, in spite of what Bill has done, Joan still loves him."

Janice approached the desks, dressed in her clean coveralls, broom in hand. Troy ignored her, sat up and continued his conversation with Hector.

"But the man is the cause of all Joan's sorrow. Killing him is the only real option." He jabbed a crooked finger. "And she should take out that Alicia bitch while she's at it. A large rock upside the head should do the trick nicely."

Janice sat on the corner of the desk. "You've been down here a long time, haven't you, Troy?"

Troy slid the chair back and stood up. He gave a curt nod in Janice's direction.

"A pleasant day to you, Janice," he said, a hint of menace in the tone. He looked back to Hector. "I shall see you later, my friend."

"Yeah, man. Next time."

Janice watched Troy leave, then dropped down into John's chair. She swung it around until she was facing Hector, her broom held out to one side.

"What's up, Janice?" asked Hector.

Janice shrugged, frowned, said nothing.

"Yeah. Same here," said Hector. He slid his chair forward and began sorting through paperwork on his desk. "How you and John getting on?"

"All right," said Janice. A thoughtful pause, then, "He say anything?"

"Nah. But he's got the look."

"What look?"

"Ya' know. The look." He glanced in her direction. "Kinda' like the one you got."

Janice gave a solemn, almost meek smile.

"Well, maybe not that one," said Hector.

"Sorry," said Janice through a soft chuckle.

"Don't worry about it." Hector smiled sympathetically. "You make a cute couple. Talk of the town."

Chapter 6

John sat alone at the same table that he and Janice used most often. There was a single mug sitting on the table before him.

The man with the newspaper was sitting at the next table, the front page facing away from him revealed the headline *'Founder's Day Today'*.

The barista behind the counter looked rather bored.

John appeared dejected.

He smiled though when Janice finally came into the café from the open tunnel.

Her manner was difficult to read at first. She might have been angry, she might have been sorrowful.

John stood as she approached the table. "Good morning, Janice," he said. "I was afraid you weren't coming."

The both sat down at the same time. Janice got the attention of the barista, who nodded and began preparing Janice's order.

"Listen," John went on, "I'm really sorry about the other night."

"No, John. It wasn't your fault. My fault. All my fault. I overreacted. I always overreact. I'm sorry."

"Well, I'm glad you're here."

"Hey, it's your first Founder's Day." Janice's words sounded forced. "Gotta give you the special tour."

"I'm looking forward to it," said John. "I have a few things to get squared away at the station, and after that I'm all yours."

The barista brought Janice her coffee. She waited until she started back to the counter.

"Of course you are, John." She turned the cup about, slowly lifted it up and took a cautious sip. She smiled thinly as she set the cup back down. "And I appreciate that. I appreciate that very much."

□ □ □ □

Janice walked down the hallway, rounded the corner and stopped.

Troy was blocking her path. He did not look happy. He had a dark, menacing look on his face.

"Get out of my way, Troy," said Janice.

"Or what?"

"Just get out of my way." Janice sounded more bored than frightened.

Troy took a step closer. "You leave him alone."

Now Janice looked startled. "What?"

"You may have played the freedom fighter topside, but down here you're just another tunnel dweller. You step out of line, you'll find yourself on the long march down the hall."

Janice's expression shifted to uncertainty. "I don't know what you're talking about."

"I won't let you take John Smith down with you," Troy said in a dark, ominous tone. "He belongs <u>here</u>. He belongs at the station."

"I would never do that to John."

"*Love*, Janice?" Troy smirked. "That happened once before, did it not?"

"I—"

"That is what got you sent down here, is it not?"

"That was different."

"Quite disturbing, if I understand correctly. Most, most unsettling."

Janice appeared crestfallen. Her tone changed to one of surrender. "I've spent a hundred years atoning for that."

"That makes everything okay, then?" Troy moved in close and had to tilt his head to look up at her. "Nothing you do here goes unnoticed. All is seen. All is heard."

He went in for the final turn. "You are watched, my little revolutionary."

Janice made a final attempt to stand up to the little man. Her words were cool and precise.

"I know that," she said.

Troy's expression oh-so-slowly morphed into cool satisfaction. He let Janice dwell on her situation a moment more, then calmly stepped around the woman and disappeared down the hall.

Alone now in the empty tunnel, unmoving, Janice looked frightened, broken. She fought against an uncontrollable trembling.

□ □ □ □

John and Hector stood in front of the television monitor. The narrator was speaking in a smooth, bold voice.

"When you can't be out there celebrating, you need to be right here with us. We'll be feeding you Founder's Day programming all day and all night."

"Yes, we will," said Hector, quite matter-of-factly.

The narrator's tone shifted then to heavy solemnity. "In keeping with the solemnness of the occasion, this afternoon we'll be bringing you a very special 'Tell it to Judge Roy'. Believe me, this is one you won't want to miss."

"No, you won't," Hector stated calmly.

The narrator's tone shifted again. "Now back to Hot Seat LeGrande, a Founder's Day edition of your show and mine, The Hot Seat!"

"And here we go," said Hector.

The Hot Seat returned, and Jim, host of The Hot Seat, was talking to Bob.

"This is it, Bob. This is your chance. Today... Founder's Day. You could win it all." Dramatic pause. "All right. You know how this works."

Hector spoke pointedly to the television.

"Give it to me, Jim."

"One more question, Bob," said Jim. "This is today's final question."

At that moment, Janice stepped up beside John. "You ready to go?"

"Uh..." John was unable to take his eyes off the television monitor.

"Uh?" asked Janice.

"Shhh," hissed Hector.

Jim on the television: "Are you ready, Bob?"

"Oh, he's ready," said Hector.

John pointed weakly up at the monitor. "One second, Janice. Bob might win."

"Hey. I'm trying to hear this," said Hector.

"Bob might win?" Janice was near to fuming. "You hate this show. You hate all these shows. We're supposed to be going to the midway."

"Just one sec," said John. "Just ... one..."

"I'm supposed to show you Founder's Day." Janice suddenly sounded more hurt than angry.

"Hey..." cried Hector. "I missed the question!"

"Janice, I promise," pleaded John. "I just want to see—"

"Okay, John," said Janice, very coolly.

She turned away.

"Janice!" John called after her as she stalked away.

"That's right, Bob!" Jim cried out. "That is absolutely right!"

There was loud, ecstatic cheering from the unseen audience.

"You have done it!" Jim continued to cry out, near screaming. "You have done it! You have taken it on! You have faced it down! And you have beaten it!"

Janice continued to stalk off.

Hector looked painfully up at the monitor. "Aw, man."

John hurried after Janice.

Hector pointed numbly up at the monitor. A sad, empty gesture.

Jim, the host of The Hot Seat, had to speak over the roaring cheers of the unseen studio audience.

"This is ab-so-lute-ly phenomenal!" he cried. "Oh, my goodness! Ladies and Gentlemen, this moment will live in KHDZ history FOR-absolutely-EVER!"

"Aw, man," said Hector.

The tunnel holding the Founder's Day midway was wider than most. This allowed for booths to line one side and still permit the crowd of people to pass comfortably through.

Several dozen people were milling about. John and Janice were among them, each with a small bag of popcorn in hand. Their body language made it very clear that Janice was in control of the situation.

They were near the 'Drown the Clowns' booth; a row of squirt guns targeting a row of clown heads. Booths further down the line included Whack-A-Joel, Cupid's Arrow and the Dunking Machine.

"D'you notice?" John was saying, "This popcorn is all right, but... it does have an odd aftertaste. Don't you think?"

Janice drifted closer to the Drown the Clowns booth.

"Consider the heat source that popped it, John,' she said absently.

John looked down at his bag and grimaced, tossed the almost full bag into a nearby trash bin.

The booth had a row of six squirt guns mounted to the counter, each corresponding to a clown head at the back of the booth. An empty balloon was sticking out of the top of each clown head.

But instead of plastic clown heads, these were real heads, real clowns.

A carnie sat in a raised chair behind the counter. He was a scruffy looking middle-aged man with a week's unshaven face.

"Come on up, people," he said, "and have a seat. Take aim, fill 'em up, bust the balloon, win your prize."

John looked apprehensively at the squirt guns. He leaned near Janice. "It is water, right?" he asked.

Janice leaned over the nearest gun. She looked up at the carnie, who wrinkled a single, caterpillar brow.

Janice cautiously touched the end of the gun with a finger, calmly rubbed the fingers together.

"Well?" asked John.

Janice sniffed at her finger, lightly touched her fingertip to her tongue.

"Janice!"

Janice looked coolly at John, finally stuck out her undamaged tongue.

The carnie shook his head and turned his attention back to the milling crowd. "Let's go folks. Take a seat, shoot the clown."

Another midway visitor sat down at a pistol station, leaving only one seat open.

Janice nudged John. "Go for it, John," she said.

John looked uncomfortably at the row of living clown heads at the back of the booth.

They looked calmly back.

"I don't think so," he said.

Janice quickly slid into the last empty seat. "Wuss." She settled in and made ready for the contest.

"We've got our six marksmen, people," said the carnie. He shifted about and placed a hand on a big red button. "Everybody ready... Everybody aim..."

He pushed the button and a metallic alarm sounded. "Everybody fire," he finished.

Janice and the others pulled the triggers of their mounted pistols. Water streamed out, striking the faces of the clowns, occasionally making it into their open mouths.

As the contest progressed, each of the clown heads sputtered and choked. The balloons protruding from the top of each slowly filled with air.

Janice called out to the clown head that she was targeting. "Keep your mouth open, Brad!"

Brad the Clown Head sputtered and choked like all the others. "Damn you, Janice," he said amid the sputtering. "You bit—"

Janice got in a good, long stream of water that choked off the end of Brad's comment.

"Open up!" she said sharply. "Open!"

There was a loud pop as the balloon atop a clown head several heads down the line from Brad popped. All the water streams faded to nothing and the balloons atop the other clown heads slowly deflated.

"Winner at station three!" said the carnie. He reached up and grabbed a small stuffed doll, tossed it to the winner.

Janice stood up, glared across at Brad the Clown Head.

"Thanks a whole lot, Brad," she said.

"Go to hell, Janice," said Brad the Clown Head.

Brad the Clown Head started laughing, and then all the Clown Heads started laughing.

The carnie rose up from his chair grinning. "All right, you clowns," he called out to his staff. "Let's try and keep it professional."

There was more laughter from the clown heads. Walking away from the booth, John was grinning but Janice did not appear pleased.

"He did that on purpose," she said.

"A friend of yours, is he?"

"No friend of mine."

The sign over the next booth read 'Whack-A- Joel'. It consisted of table with eight holes cut into the top, each large enough to fit a head through. A big, burly carnie stood behind the table, arms folded, a wooden mallet held in one hand.

Janice looked down at the table, then up at the burly carnie. "Where's Joel?" she asked.

"He's in there," said the burly carnie. He sounded bored.

Joel poked his head up through one of the holes. Janice smiled down at him.

"Hello, Joel."

"Hello, Janice," said Joel

A second head, also Joel, popped up through another hole in the table. "Hey, Janice," he said.

A third Joel Head popped up through yet another. "Janice!"

"Hello, Joel," said Janice. Then, "Hello, Joel."

John looked ill at ease, and perhaps a little queasy, as he eyed the collection of Joels. Still, he tried his best to maintain his composure.

"Do you know everybody here?" he asked Janice.

Yet another Joel popped up and smiled happily up at Janice.

Janice smiled back at the latest Joel. She held her hand out to the burly carnie, who handed her the wooden mallet. She looked down at the table. Eight Joel Heads, one in each hole, were smiling up at her.

"You guys ready?" she asked.

"Ready!" said all the Joel Heads.

"Let's do this."

All eight heads dropped down into their holes.

Janice readied herself. She bent her knees slightly, held the mallet at the ready. She glanced briefly up at the burly carnie, then focused her attention on the tabletop.

She nodded curtly. With that, the carnie unemotionally lowered a hand down on his big red button.

The Joel Heads started popping up through the openings, one at a time. Each stayed up for less than a second before dropping down again.

Janice began whacking them on the head with the wooden mallet.

The Joels began popping up and dropping down more and more quickly. Janice whacked them more and more quickly, the action growing faster and faster.

John and Janice climbed into a colorful cart that was sitting outside a tunnel entrance. Above the entrance was a sign that read 'Tunnel of Love'.

Once settled into the cart, it started forward and slowly disappeared into the darkness within.

The cart came out of the tunnel a few moments later.

John hurriedly jumped out even before the cart could come to a complete stop. He looked anxiously, and with some panic, horror, and utter disbelief, back at the tunnel.

Janice was laughing gleefully.

John and Janice stood in front of an elaborately constructed Dunking Machine. Janice prepared to throw a red ball at the target that was hanging beside a terrified looking woman sitting on the drop shelf.

Five or six others stood about, all eagerly watching and waiting.

John stepped up to the half-wall that encircled the dunking machine. He looked down into the pit that the victim would be dropped into if Janice hit the target.

Janice threw the first ball... and just missed. Several in the crowd groaned. Several others threw up their arms in frustration.

John looked up at a sign that hung on a post beside the machine: "Drop her into the Pit of Despair".

Janice threw the second ball. The ball hit the target. The victim dropped into the Pit of Despair, disappearing quickly from sight.

The small crowd went crazy, dancing and cheering. Janice jumped up and down triumphantly.

John caught a quick glimpse of Debbie. She stood unmoving amongst the cheering, dancing crowd.

John glanced hesitantly over the half-wall and down into the pit.

Looking up again, away from the pit, into the crowd... Debbie was gone.

John and Janice sat at their favorite table in the café, each now with a personalized mug. For the first time, all the other tables were occupied, and there were several people standing at the counter.

John looked as though he wanted to be having a good time, and for Janice's sake was trying to appear as though he was actually having a good time. Coming through this false front that he was putting up was the fact that he just didn't get it.

Janice, on the other hand, looked to be really enjoying the day.

"I think this year's boat race may be the best I've seen," she said. "And I've seen my share."

She watched John struggle with a smile. "You don't think so?" she asked.

"You can't go by me, Janice. My first year."

"But you ought to know if you liked it or not."

John struggled to come up with a satisfactory answer, or at least a safe one. "It was pretty good, I guess," he said at last. "I mean, maybe it really wasn't my kind of thing, ya' know?"

"How can you say that?" Janice was perplexed. "It had everything. Wild fans, suspense, seat-of-the-pants thrills."

"Of course. You're right..." said John. "You're right..."

Janice studied John suspiciously. "You didn't like it at all."

"It was fine." John surrendered under the pressure. "I'm sorry, it's just... Janice, it was six people hurtling their boats at full speed into a wall. First one to splat wins."

Janice looked stricken. "What about the Cupid's Arrow booth?"

John was obviously afraid to answer, but finally, grudgingly, "You shot that girl in the heart with an arrow."

"John," she stated defensively. "I begged you to be my target."

"Yes! To be shot in the heart with an arrow!"

"And you would have loved me forever!"

"I don't need to be shot with an arrow to love you, Janice."

"Oh, how sweet..."

John stared down at his personalized mug.

"And that girl?" he asked.

Janice picked up her own mug and took a long drink, finally set the cup carefully back onto the table, turned it label out.

"She'll love me forever, of course," she said softly.

"You're okay with that?" When Janice doesn't answer right away, he asked another question. "You're okay with all of this?"

Janice looked uncomfortable; really uncomfortable for perhaps the first time. It took a long time for her to answer.

"It's all in fun, John," she said, a bit guiltily. "I mean, ya' gotta give us something."

"Janice, I—"

"I accept where I am. I deserve to be here. I know that. We all deserve to be here."

"I—"

"But I gotta push back," Janice cut him off. "I have to. I have to resist. It's just... it's who I am."

"I can see that," he said. "I'm all right with that. But what does it have to do with Founder's Day?"

"Nothing," Janice admitted. "Not really. But it does. It all does. Everything does. It's all the same thing."

"I don't understand."

"I know." A melancholy smile. "I think that's why I'm drawn to you."

Now John had to smile. "I like you, too."

Janice leaned back in her chair and grew introspective. Her words were spoken as if to herself.

"There is no winning, here," she said. "There is no fight, really. The most you can do is struggle against the ties. That's what I do. I resist, even knowing that in the end... in the end, we are where we are."

She struggled with a silent, internal demon. Her tone then was one of acceptance. "But that's not you, though. Is it?"

John spoke fretfully, words stumbling. "I'm just here until—"

"Yeah, I know," said Janice. "Paperwork."

The viewing stand was a raised wooden platform, eight feet by ten feet, with wooden rails that had been decorated with colorful paper streamers. In the center of the platform were two chairs. Sitting in the chairs were the announcers for the Parade of Souls: the Mayor and Mike Johansen.

They were broadcasting the parade to the television audience. Each held a microphone. As always, there were no cameras visible.

"Mr. Mayor," said Mike Johansen. "If what I've seen so far of this year's Founder's Day is any indication of what to expect here, the Parade of Souls promises to really be something special."

"Absolutely, Mike. Everyone involved in this year's celebration receives a hearty *'well done'* from me," said the Mayor. "But then, I expected no less. I believe I stated on your very program that this would be the best year ever."

"You certainly did," Mike smiled and shook his head dramatically. "I must admit, though, with some of the great Founder's Days I've experienced in past years, I seriously doubted that you could pull it off. My hat is off to you, sir. A superb job."

"Thank you, Mike."

"So, with the parade set to begin at any moment, what can we expect?"

"Surprises, Mike. Thrills, chills... and surprises."

John and Janice approached Miss Constance's 'Up All Night' booth. Her purple couch was there, positioned beneath a colorful silk canopy. Miss Constance was lounging comfortably, and a line of fans waited anxiously to approach, small pieces of paper held tightly in hand.

Miss Constance playfully inspected each fan that stepped forward and apprehensively deposited their strip of paper into a large glass jar.

She smiled demurely when she saw John and Janice watching from out in the midway. She lifted a hand and wiggled her fingers in an inviting hello.

John lifted a hand to wave back, but Janice tugged at his arm and dragged him along. The two of them continued down the midway, but John did manage one more curious look back.

Miss Constance was waiting. She gave him a playful wink, then turned her attention back to the line, contentedly continued attending her adoring admirers.

□ □ □ □

Mike Johansen and the Mayor looked expectantly to the parade route. There was movement at the far end of the wide, high-ceilinged tunnel, and they could hear the sounds of an appreciative crowd of spectators.

It had begun.

"Mike," said the Mayor. "This year our Parade of Souls is led by a virtual 'royal court' of colorfully dressed jesters. Upon reaching their destination, the gates will open to the sounds of gaiety."

The parade route, decorated with bright streamers and banners, was lined on either side by dozens of spectators. Leading the parade were a dozen men and women dressed in colorful jester costumes. As they traveled the route, they danced and laughed and waved to the spectators.

John and Janice moved through the crowd and approached the sideline. Janice clapped happily, her face glowing as a child seeing her first parade. She waved excitedly when she saw someone among the jesters whom she recognized.

"Looking good, Darren!" she called out.

Darren the Jester waved a hearty hello to Janice, shook the balls on his hat and continued marching.

Janice continued clapping as Darren led the way for the rest of the parade as it progressed forward.

Something happened, then...

Janice's expression slowly darkened... Her clapping slowed... Her smile faded until finally her face showed no emotion at all.

She spoke softly. "Wait for me."

John could only just hear her over the background noise of the crowd. He wasn't really certain that he understood what she said, but before he could respond, she turned and walked away.

John was left to watch her disappear into the crowd.

Mike Johansen and the Mayor continued to broadcast the parade to their unseen television audience, through the as always unseen cameras.

"Wonderful, Mr. Mayor," said Mike. "Just wonderful."

The mayor wore a bright grin. "It is just the beginning, Mike. Just the beginning."

Mike straightened suddenly. This was... this something completely unexpected.

"What is this? Am I seeing things?"

The Mayor beamed proudly, barely managing to keep his silence, to allow the sight itself to speak for itself.

"Mr. Mayor. Is that... is that Bob?"

"That's right, Mike," the Mayor said at last. "A favorite of yours, I do believe. This year's King of the Parade of Souls; on his way to an existence that we can only imagine."

"Oh, a splendid choice, Mr. Mayor," whispered Mike.

John watched from the sidelines.

Four men in leather harnesses, bound together by thick ropes, pulled a large, wooden cart. The wheels of the flat cart were four feet in diameter and made of solid wood. The heavy wheels ground noisily over the gritty floor of the tunnel.

Bob from the Hot Seat television program sat atop the flatbed cart in a large, high-back chair: a cheap throne. He wore a paper crown and held a wooden scepter in one hand.

He smiled and waved to the crowd with his free hand.

The cheering crowd called out to him.

"Bob, Bob!"

"We love you, Bob!"

"I wanna have your baby, Bob!"

John was distracted, anxious, his attention drawn more to the crowd than the spectacle of the King of the Parade of Souls.

He searched the crowd for any sign of Janice.

The sound of Mike and the Mayor speaking, then.

"And now, Mike, and to all of you who couldn't be with us today, I bring you... the Lost Souls."

Behind Bob's cart walked a somber gathering of men and women. Each had a haunted expression, and empty gaze. They plodded slowly forward, oblivious to those who watched.

And those who watched grew solemn and quiet. Those who wore hats took them off.

"A humbling sight, dear sir," came Mike's voice.

The Mayor's voice again. "May those who walk before us today find peace where they tread tomorrow."

"Well said, Mr. Mayor."

A moment later, the expression on John Smith's face turned to bewilderment.

Amongst the lost souls walked Janice, following behind the King of the Lost Souls. As all the others, she was oblivious to those around her.

John pushed between the two people standing in front of him. "Janice! Janice!"

Janice didn't respond.

John stepped out in front of the crowd.

The spindly arms of Troy reached out and grasped tightly to John.

John didn't seem to notice. "Janice! No! Janice!"

The tiny figure of Troy stepped fully beside John.

"No, John Smith." Troy pulled John backward.

"Janice!" John struggled to free himself from the little creature, to get to Janice. "This isn't right! Janice! I have to—"

"No, John Smith," Troy said sternly.

"But—" John looked desperately at Troy.

"You cannot," said Troy. "She is lost to us. They are all lost to us, now."

John looked from the Parade of Souls to Troy and back, frantic to do something, anything...

The last of the souls passed.

"You are safe, John Smith," said Troy.

"What?" John turned sharply to Troy.

"You belong <u>here</u>."

As John looked down at the little creature, trying to sort out what Troy meant, the sound of Mike Johansen's somber, respectful voice could be heard.

"What an amazing sight, Mr. Mayor. Stunning. I find myself speechless." More chipper, then. "And I do believe there are a record number of participants this year."

Chapter 7

The station floor was dimly aglow, illuminated only by the light of the 'Up All Night' program set at the far end of the cavern, where Miss Constance was being doing her show.

John couldn't hear her from where he sat, alone at his desk. He leaned back in his chair, stared out across the room, lost in thought and absently fumbling with a pencil.

Mr. Henderson saw John when he came into the station.

"A long day, Mr. Smith." Mr. Henderson cleared one corner of John's desk and sat.

John put on a melancholy half smile without looking up. "Most definitely a long day, Mr. Henderson."

Mr. Henderson gave John a long, understanding gaze.

"It's been quite some time since my own, but I do see it in others," he said.

"What's that?" John absently tossed the pencil onto the desk.

"Your first Founder's Day." Mr. Henderson paused, looked across the cavern at Miss Constance, who was joyfully going about her show. He continued then without looking down at John. "It can be a traumatic experience, one's first."

"It doesn't make any sense."

"I don't think it's supposed to make sense, John."

John looked up at Mr. Henderson for the first time. "People actually enjoy it?"

"This is Hades, son. We're not meant to enjoy anything."

"Janice seemed to think so."

"That a fact." The statement was noncommittal.

"It's all in fun," John quoted. "That's what she said. You have to give us something."

Mr. Henderson looked away from John, a peculiar grin forming on his face.

"Janice was never one to open herself up to people, but with you, she was trying." His tone turned darkly serious. "Founder's Day is a game, my young friend. A very serious, very emotionally manipulative game."

Mr. Henderson stood, straightened the items on the desk that he had pushed aside.

"Yes, it is all '*in fun*'." He nodded toward Mr. Horn's office. "His. Not ours. Everything you saw today, was driven by him, was for his benefit."

"He's not even here."

"He is always here." Dead calm then. "Don't you ever doubt that."

John Smith visibly struggled to sort out what this all meant.

"What was it all about? What is any of this about?"

"We can never know what he's trying to accomplish. That's all part of what he's here. What we try to do is play against that." Mr. Henderson was speaking more as a professor than a station manager now. "This reality may have been his design, but we took it and wrapped it all up in a pretty package. We do our best to turn it in on itself; as much as he'll let us, and maybe just a little bit more. How else could we possibly get through it, year after year?"

"And the parade?"

"The reason for Founder's Day. The grand culmination of all that comes before it." Mr. Henderson held up a hand. "Before you ask, I have no idea how the Lost Souls are chosen. Sometime during the parade, they just... *know*. It could happen to any of us. Each year, it might be any one of us."

"What happens to them?"

"No one has ever come back, so no one really knows."

"Some place worse than..." John couldn't finish.

"Who's to say?"

"Then how do you know it's not a way out of here?"

"I don't. One can hope."

Mr. Henderson started away from John's desk, but turned back after a few steps. "Janice rule number four. Never talk about what underlies Founder's Day. Doing so would burst the bubble."

He turned and continued away, spoke over his shoulder. "*You gotta give us something...*"

□ □ □ □

A thin mist hung in John's cell, the last remnants of his earlier shower. He could be heard in the bathroom beyond the threshold as he prepared for the day.

The television on the dresser in the main room was turned on. The morning newscaster was reporting on the previous day's Founder's Day celebration.

"Thank you very much for that thoughtful report, Jeff. An interesting story that should not be lost in all the excitement of yesterday's myriad of Founder's Day activities."

He focused then on the audience and the next of the Founder's Day stories. "By all accounts, this year's celebration was the finest we've had in these parts in a long, long time. This from the mayor late last evening."

The Mayor's voice came over the tiny speaker of the television. "In every respect but one, this is without a doubt the most thrilling Founder's Day in all my years as mayor."

"He was referring, of course, to the absence once again of Mr. Horn," said the newscaster. "The mayor went on to express his sincere hope that the busy founder will be able to attend next year." A change in tone then, as he continued through the stories. "As every year, the grand finale of yesterday's numerous events was the Parade of Souls. Procession-goers were witness to a record ninety six participants, several from right here in the KHDZ studios."

After a moment's hesitation, "We wish them all the best."

There was a knock at the door. John came out of the bathroom buttoning his shirt. His hair was still wet and was combed straight back.

The newscaster continued unabated. "In other related news, three participants in this year's boat race—"

John reached over and turned off the television, shutting down the newscaster's voice with a loud click.

He opened the door. Troy stood in the hallway.

"Troy... good morning." John stepped aside. "Come in."

"No thank you, John Smith." Troy sounded as somber as John felt. "I bring you a message."

They stared at one another for a long moment.

"So..." John said finally. "The message?"

Troy gave a half-bow. "Your presence is required at the station."

"All right. I—"

Before he could finish his sentence, Troy turned precisely and left, stalking stiffly away on his thin, spindly legs. John watched after the little creature, then slowly closed the door.

□ □ □ □

Hector sat at his desk, attentively watching the television mounted on the far wall. He glanced very briefly at the approaching John Smith before returning his full attention to the news program. The newscaster's words and tone and turned cool and professional.

"We are unable to verify exactly when he arrived," said the newscaster. "But it is believed to have been sometime late last night and, as is his custom, he returned to us without fanfare. Once again, this late-breaking news; Mr. Horn returned sometime late last night."

Hector spoke calmly to John without looking at him. "You really shouldn't keep him waiting."

"I don't know what—" John stood beside his desk. "I was just told that—"

Hector lifted an arm and pointed in the general direction of Mr. Horn's office.

John tried not to look at the heavy plank door. "You mean—"

Hector used the remote to turn down the volume on the television, returned to the paperwork on his desk.

"Yep," he stated quietly.

The walls of Mr. Horn's large office were covered in thick panels of rich, dark woods. A large, heavy desk was at the far end of the room facing the door.

There was a solid knock on the door.

An oddly familiar voice responded to the knock.

"Come in," said Mr. Horn.

The door opened and John Smith stepped hesitantly into the room. There was a heavy, hollow thud sound when he closed the door behind him. He was confused when he saw who looked like a well-dressed Nicolas Cage sitting behind the desk.

"I'm sorry. I was looking for Mr. Horn." John stumbled over his words.

"Hello, Mr. Smith. Please. Sit down."

"Aren't you... but you... I didn't even know you were, you know... wow. You're down <u>here</u>?"

John's attention was drawn to a long, leathery, barbed tail curled around the side of the desk. Mr. Horn smiled thinly and the tail slid back out of view.

"Is it all right if I call you John?" He indicated the guest chair.

"Please, John. Do sit."

John again fumbled for words as he sat in the offered chair.

"But aren't you—"

"Call me Mr. Horn." Mr. Horn / Nicolas Cage smiled brightly and leaned back in his maroon-colored leather chair.

"John," he continued. "I would like very much for us to start out on the right foot. How about you? Wouldn't you like for us to start out on the right foot?"

John nodded numbly but said nothing.

"Good, good. After all, the situation in which you and I find ourselves is no reason for us to be less than civil with one another, is it?"

"No."

"Very good. I'm so glad you agree."

"Yes, sir."

Mr. Horn, wearing a perfectly charming expression, carefully studied his guest.

"It must have been a helluva shocker, finding yourself down here. Eh?"

"Yes," said John. "It certainly was."

"With your fine record. Teaching our troubled youth, no less. And all that volunteer work!"

Mr. Horn leaned forward and placed his forearms on his desk. He clasped his hands together.

"Yet, here we are. All to the good, from my side of the ledger. A soul on the books that I wouldn't ordinarily have, a new set of eyes here at the station; and, from what I hear, a damned fine producer for one of my favorite programs." Another broad smile. "Great, eh?"

"S'pose so."

"Oh, come now, John. Don't be glum. It could have been so much worse, could it not?"

"So I hear."

"My, yes. You could have been sent... " Mr. Horn used his fingers in an exaggerated air quote gesture. "*down the hall*, as they like to say around here."

"Yes." John mumbled almost silently.

"You would have been miserable, John, and I would never have had the benefit of your expertise as producer of Miss Constance' fine television program. So." Another bright smile. "We both win. Right? Everyone wins. Eh?"

"I guess so."

"You guess so? John, John." He spoke earnestly. "Show me the error in my logic."

"I'm not supposed to be here."

Mr. Horn's tone grew no-nonsense and more stern. "But you are here. That is a fact, my friend. I can see you. You are sitting right in front of me. Is that not so?"

"Yes."

"I can do nothing to change that. You can do nothing to change that. It is completely out of our hands. We must make do, as best we can, until the Powers That Be see fit to correct their little mistake."

There was a long pause, and when Mr. Horn / Nicolas Cage spoke again, it was with a firm finality. "So. John Smith. Welcome to the KHDZ family. If there is anything that I can do to make your time with us more... agreeable... please do not hesitate to ask."

The conversation was unmistakably at an end.

John Smith heard the slithering sound of Mr. Horn's tail sliding across the floor. Mr. Horn continued to hold his charming, shining smile.

John stood up with some uncertainty.

"Yes, sir." John walked toward the door. He stopped midway across the room and turned about to face the figure of Nicolas Cage sitting at the large desk.

"Mr. Horn?"

"Yes, John?" Mr. Horn leaned back comfortably.

"The parade... the Parade of Souls."

"Yes, John." He looked as though the very mention of the event gave him tremendous pleasure.

"Where do they go? The Lost Souls."

"Oh, John," Mr. Horn offered a gentle smile. "To a very, very special place."

John waited a moment more, hoping for more of an answer. There was nothing more.

"Yes, sir." John started toward the door again. He reached it. He opened it.

Nicolas Cage spoke to the receding figure...

"Good day to you, John."

"Yes, sir."

Hector shifted paperwork around on his desk and looked askance at John Smith as he sat slowly down in his chair.

"Everything all right?"

John shrugged in answer. He looked dazed. He finally reached down to a cardboard box sitting on the floor beside him and set it on the desk.

The words "Really Bad Movies" were handwritten on the side. They had been written with a feminine hand.

Hector couldn't help but smile. He nodded at the box.

"Janice did that," he said.

"What?" John sounded numb, lost.

"That." Hector pointed at the box. "She wrote that."

John turned the box around and saw what Janice had written.

Hector's expression turned sympathetic. "Hey, man. You never know."

John nodded imperceptibly. He took a handful of DVDs out and set them on the desk, then set the box back on the floor.

"Hector?" he asked. "Mr. Horn..."

"Yeah?"

"He was... an actor. He was... Nicolas Cage."

"Oh. That." Hector leaned cozily back in his chair and rolled his pencil between his fingers. "I don't know this Nicolas Cage guy, but I can say with confidence that our Mr. Horn is not Nicolas Cage."

"Okay. But he—"

"A while back, a guy said Mr. Horn was someone named Angelina Jolie. Again. I wouldn't know. Me, I've seen him as Napoleon, Andrew Jackson, a lot of people." He sat forward again. "Just something he does. Someday you'll walk into his office and you'll be looking at you."

Hector returned to his work.

John looked distractedly at the DVDs on his desk. He was unable to bring himself to delve back into it.

"Listen, man," said Hector. "He's been observing us for thousands of years. He studies how we think, how we deal with problems, how we relate to one another. What we argue about."

He gave a guarded glance to Mr. Horn's door.

"I don't think he'll ever figure us out. He's too different from us." He tapped at his temple. "His mind doesn't work like ours."

"But what's with—"

"Hell, I don't know. Maybe he thinks that if he looks like us, sounds like us, that he can understand us. Who knows? Maybe he just likes dressing up in our clothes." He turned his attention to his work for good. "What's to figure? We're just here to play the game, man."

"Right," John said under his breath. "The game."

He looked away from Hector when he sensed movement across the room.

Debbie came into the station from the hall. She was dressed in clean coveralls and was carrying Janice's broom.

She looked across the room at John. After a long moment, each offered the other a slow, sad smile.

John returned to his stack of DVDs.

He had to find a movie for tonight's show.

Chapter 8

One Hundred Years Later

Maria Cordoba sat in one of the two chairs in the waiting area outside the office of the station manager. There was a manila folder in her lap. She looked out of place here and a little uncomfortable.

Troy sat in the other chair. He crossed his impossibly thin, spindly legs. He smiled at Maria. It was a friendly smile.

It nonetheless made Maria even more uncomfortable, but she managed an awkward smile in response.

Troy finally broke the silence.

"Helluva day, eh?"

Maria attempted another smile. She was only partially successful.

"It could have gone better," she said.

Troy nodded slowly, knowingly. He let out a long, drawn out sigh.

"Ah... yep."

Maria looked anxiously toward at the station manager's door, as if silently willing it to open.

Stenciled on the frosted glass inset in the door were the words *"John Smith Station Manager"*.

"You'll like him," said Troy.

"Excuse me?" Maria had a frightened, confused look on her face.

Troy pointed a long, crooked finger at John Smith's office door. "John Smith," he said. "Good man."

"Oh."

"Been at this a long time." Troy nodded sagely. "Knows his stuff. He'll take good care of you."

Maria didn't have a clue as to how to respond.

"Thank you," she said.

The station manager's door opened.

John Smith stuck his head through the opening. When he saw Maria, he stepped fully out of his office. He looked at Maria with some sense of puzzlement.

"Who are you?" he asked.

Maria stood up. "Maria. Maria Cordoba."

"That a fact," John Smith stated flatly. Seeing the folder, he held out a hand and she handed it to him.

John spoke to Troy as he opened the folder to look at the contents.

"Don't you have work to do?" he asked.

End

Made in the USA
San Bernardino, CA
27 April 2014